To Christina
with Love
Gramma and Grampa
Christmas 1987

For Shiona

First edition for the United States, Canada, and
the Philippines published 1987 by Barron's
Educational Series, Inc.

First published 1987 by Piccadilly Press Limited,
London, England

All inquiries should be addressed to:
Barron's Educational Series, Inc.
250 Wireless Boulevard
Hauppauge, New York   11788
Library of Congress Catalog Card No. 86-32043

International Standard Book No. 0-8120-5775-9

Library of Congress Cataloging-in-Publication Data

Tyrrell, Anne.
  Elizabeth Jane gets dressed.

  Summary: Presents in rhyme the trials and tribulations
of a three-year-old who is learning to dress herself.
  [1. Clothing and dress – Fiction.   2. Stories in
rhyme]   I. Castle, Caroline, ill.   II. Title.
PZ8.3.T857E1   1987   [E]   86-32043
ISBN 0-8120-5775-9

Printed in Great Britain

789   9697   987654321

ELIZABETH JANE
Gets Dressed

Anne Tyrrell
Illustrated by Caroline Castle

BARRON'S
New York · Toronto

On Monday morning Elizabeth Jane
Says that she's dressing herself again.
"But Elizabeth Jane," I say, "you're slow!
I'll have to help you a bit you know."

But Elizabeth Jane, who's practically three,
Says, "I'll do it myself. Leave it to me."

Elizabeth Jane has a sudden doubt.
Maybe her dress is inside out?
It's over her head. Is she trying to hide?
No, Elizabeth Jane is stuck inside.

Elizabeth Jane will have it her way.
She'll dress herself if it takes all day.

On Tuesday morning we search around.
Elizabeth Jane cannot be found.
She should have dressed but she hasn't tried.
She's under the bed where she thinks she'll hide.

When Elizabeth Jane at last appears
My very best hat I see she wears.

On Wednesday morning she's doing fine.
Elizabeth Jane is right on time.

How cross she'd be if only she knew
One shoe's red and the other is blue.
But Elizabeth Jane is feeling proud.
"I did it myself," she shouts aloud.

It's Thursday now and it's after eight.
"Hurry Elizabeth Jane, you're late."
Around the room Elizabeth goes
And out of the window throws her clothes.

"I won't get dressed," cries Elizabeth Jane.
"I'm not going to wear any clothes again."

On Friday morning she's naughty, too.
"Elizabeth Jane, I'm so cross with you.
You must dress early tomorrow morning.
Or I'll dress you, that's a final warning."

Elizabeth Jane smiles charmingly.
(She's a little bit sorry—it seems to me.)

While it's still dark I wake in bed.
Someone is standing by my head.
Who can it be? You'll never guess!
Elizabeth Jane in her party dress.

Elizabeth Jane says, "Look at me.
You said dress early—I did you see."

On Saturday morning I hear a shout.
"The door is stuck, and I can't get out."
"Elizabeth Jane, it's quite O.K.
Just turn the handle the other way."

She's out and dressing before too long.
I can tell by the noise that something's wrong.
Elizabeth Jane's in a towering rage.
She hates those buttons. They take an age!

On Sunday Elizabeth Jane was good.
She dressed herself (and I knew she could).
In a nice new dress—she looks so sweet,
And most amazingly clean and neat.

The rain has stopped. It's a lovely day.
Elizabeth Jane goes out to play.

She's riding her tricycle really fast.
She shouts at me as she pedals past,
"I can easily steer with one hand, you see.
I'm doing it now. Just look at me!"

Close to a puddle she's had a crash.
Elizabeth Jane has gone in, SPLASH!

Elizabeth Jane, who's nearly three,
Is covered with mud, as you can see.

What can you do with Elizabeth Jane
But get her to bathe and dress again?

But she's back already—she wasn't long.
She's washed and changed and the mud has gone.
And all by herself—oh, isn't she clever!
She'll dress herself now for ever and ever.

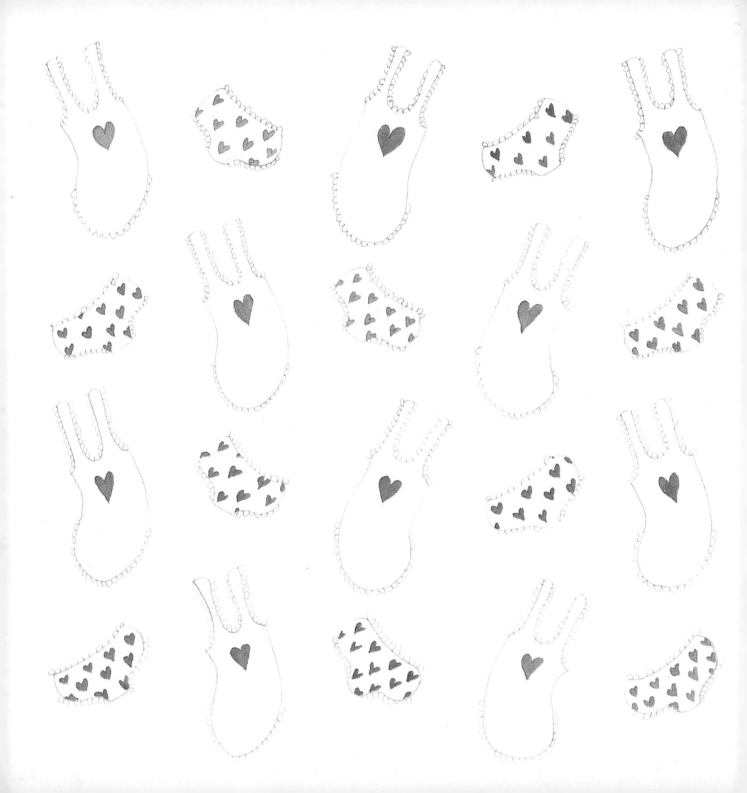